Best Friend

Story by Melaina Faranda

Illustrations by Caitlin O'Dwyer

Contents

Chapter 1

Fragile

"I wish I could help," Mum sighed, shifting on the couch. A magazine with another half-finished crossword puzzle slipped to the floor beside her.

Jet instantly dived to retrieve it for her. "I'll be okay," he said. He then repeated what Aunty Lisa always said. "You just need to concentrate on getting well."

He taped up another cardboard box, and with a black marker scrawled: *bowls and plates.*

The first time they had moved, Jet had turned each packing box into a gigantic cartoon, drawing stick figures on skateboards and marking all the boxes with his own tag, *JKB*, in bubbly lettering. Back then, it had been an adventure. And Dad had still been in their lives.

Now Dad's time was taken up with his new girlfriend, Tamara, and their baby. The "see you every other day" thing had become a weekly visit, which had turned into a weekly phone call. A call that became increasingly silent and awkward with all the things Jet couldn't say. *Why did you leave us, Dad? How could you do that when Mum is so sick? Did you really think that buying me this expensive phone was going to make it all okay?*

So, Jet stopped answering Dad's calls.

The truth was, even though Jet said he'd be okay, that was just something he *had* to say. From the start, no one had asked Jet what he truly thought. How he felt about Dad going. Or, the first time they'd moved, how he felt about leaving the house he'd known and lived in all his life. A house with a bike track that ran along the back and friends who lived on the same street.

Instead, he and Mum had moved into a tiny apartment with a single balcony, choked with traffic fumes from the busy street below.

And now they were moving again – to one of those half-houses, joined in a row to others that all looked the same. A "townhouse", Aunty Lisa called it.

Aunty Lisa had explained to Jet that Mum needed to live near the hospital. It was too expensive for her to keep relying on taxis. And because the area was all newly built, he'd go to a great new school and make great new friends.

Jet didn't want to go to another new school. This would be his third in less than a year. He didn't want to make new friends. He already had friends – friends who knew about Mum. How was he going to explain to anyone new about her? The reasons why she was always lying on the couch, or suddenly having to be rushed to the hospital.

Instead of saying any of this, Jet pretended to be okay. He didn't have a choice.

Feeling a surge of guilt, he asked, "Do you need anything, Mum?"

Mum was roused from where she had started to doze. She smiled and shook her head.

"What did I do to deserve you?" Mum asked. Her voice sounded cracked and weak. "I'm the luckiest woman in the world."

Jet checked to see that there were still tablets in the pack next to her glass of water.

Lucky? Living like this! While Dad got to live near the beach with someone who still laughed at his silly jokes. Someone who didn't need looking after. Someone who wasn't sick.

On the side of the packing box, Jet savagely scrawled: *FRAGILE.*

Chapter 2

No One Home

"And this is the library," Oliver said, winding up the whirlwind tour before bringing Jet back to class.

Jet nodded, barely bothering to look. He was scanning for a quieter place, somewhere hidden away, where he'd be able to spend his lunch-time.

The teacher had sat Jet next to Oliver and asked Oliver to be his buddy over the next week or so. Although Oliver had agreed cheerfully enough, Jet didn't want to talk. Or, at least, it wasn't so much that he didn't want to talk, it was more that he had nothing to say.

If he started talking, Oliver would ask questions. That's just what people did. And it was the last thing Jet wanted. He didn't want anyone knowing about Mum. He had made Aunty Lisa promise she wouldn't say anything when she dropped him at his new school that morning.

"Jet?" Ms Pinta was right next to his desk. She waved her hand in front of his eyes. "Is anyone at home?"

Startled, Jet jumped and knocked his pencils off the table. As they went skittering across the floor, the class erupted into laughter. He scrambled to collect them.

The teacher's voice became softer. "Jet, I asked if you could please get your maths workbook out. We're moving on."

He searched through the things on his desk for the right workbook.

The night before, Mum had watched him from the couch as he'd sat and covered each workbook with clear sticky paper.

"I used to do that for you," she'd said with a sad smile.

Jet had done his best to smile back as he held up a crinkled cover, complete with bumps and air bubbles. "Way better than when I do it!" he said.

They were still surrounded by boxes. Aunty Lisa had promised she'd be over on the weekend to help sort where things should go. The TV still had to be connected, so there wasn't even the comforting sound of voices in the background.

That night, after hardly touching the Thai curry Jet had microwaved for her, Mum dozed on the couch.

Jet made up her bed, using her favourite quilt cover with the palm trees and flamingos. Aunty Lisa had sent a bunch of bright red flowers, which he put in a glass of water on the chest of drawers facing Mum's bed.

But even all that colour couldn't overcome the bleak, empty feeling in the house. And deeper still, the slow cold burning sensation in Jet's gut.

When Dad called, Jet switched his phone to silent.

Chapter 3

Principal's Office

“Jet!”

Ms Pinta pointed to the whiteboard. “That’s the third time I’ve asked you to start writing before I move on.”

Jet felt like shrugging. Instead he said, “Sorry,” without really meaning it.

The teacher sighed. “Jet, I know you’re new to this school and there’s a lot to take in, but it’s been a couple of weeks now. Unless you participate, you’ll fall behind. Sorry isn’t good enough. You can stay in with me at lunch-time to catch up. Actions have consequences.”

“Yeah, whatever.”

Ms Pinta’s eyebrows raised. “Excuse me! Did I just hear that correctly?”

The class fell silent, waiting.

Jet nodded wearily. He was tired after a night of bad dreams and hearing Mum get up and down, sometimes groaning with pain. And none of this meant anything anyway. Ms Pinta could dish out any “consequence” that she wanted to.

Jet just wanted Ms Pinta to leave him alone.

"I said, *whatever.*"

"Okay, I've had enough of this rudeness," said Ms Pinta. "If you can't listen to what I'm saying and follow instructions, then I'd like you to go to the office, please. Perhaps you would prefer to explain your behaviour to the principal."

As he waited for the principal, Jet fidgeted with the button on his shirt, his heart pounding beneath his fingers. What if Ms Ravel got angry with him and gave him a lunch-time detention? What if she told Mum? He wished he hadn't been rude to his teacher. The last thing he wanted was for Mum to worry even more than she already did.

"Jet?"

Jet was surprised to see that Ms Ravel was smiling. It seemed like a genuinely friendly smile. Then again, thinking about Dad and Aunty Lisa and any number of doctors, Jet knew that sometimes adults smiled like that before they delivered bad news.

"How are you settling in, then?" she asked.

Jet gulped. "Um, I, uh, okay. I mean, um, Ms Pinta sent me here because I didn't get all the writing done."

Ms Ravel nodded. "Is there a reason for that?"

MS RAVEL

Jet stared. How could he begin to explain? Although Aunty Lisa and Mum always talked about Mum getting better, Jet had caught the flicker of a shadow in Aunty Lisa's eyes. The thing that was not being said. Compared to that, nothing else seemed to be important.

Who cared what happened back in dusty old ancient Egypt, or how to draw and label a diagram of a leaf? Who cared about trying to get to know people, or making new friends, when it could all be taken away again by yet another house move?

But how could Jet express any of this to Ms Ravel? Or how hard he found it to just concentrate, or the constant burning he felt in his stomach?

"I guess I'm just tired," he said.

"Why might that be? Are you getting enough sleep?" The principal gave an exaggerated roll of her eyes. "Don't tell me – you kids and your devices."

Jet pretended to smile, as if she'd guessed correctly.

Ms Ravel nodded again, but now her smile became serious. "Jet, I'd like to suggest you see our school counsellor, Tim. He's a good guy, and I get the feeling that you and he might have some things in common."

Jet shook his head. No way did he want to have to talk about stuff with a counsellor. It would be like in the movies where he'd be asked a bunch of questions about his feelings. He wasn't going to reveal the truth about Mum – about any of it. He needed to stay strong.

Ms Ravel's gentle smile became firmer. "I'm afraid I'm not really offering you a choice, Jet, although I might have made it seem that way. We have a zero-tolerance policy on rudeness to our teachers at this school. You either see the counsellor, or I'll have to speak with your mother."

Chapter 4

Waiting for the Storm to Pass

Jet glanced about the counsellor's office. On a small, low table sat a sand tray with some mini-figures and plastic dinosaurs on it. There was a tub of crayons, and some books and folders. Bright posters were stuck up all over the windows with sayings like: *Be Who You Are; You Matter; Don't Let Anyone Dull Your Sparkle; Life Isn't About Waiting for the Storm to Pass – It's About Learning to Dance in the Rain.*

The counsellor saw Jet roll his eyes and smiled. "Choose your seat, but just a tip – I'd definitely grab the couch if I were you."

Jet sat back on a fire-engine red couch with sky-and-cloud-patterned cushions. From there, between a gap in the posters, he could see a bright green sliver of the park beyond the tall bars of the school fence.

"So, Jet, welcome! I'm Tim, and I believe we're here because of a misunderstanding in the classroom. Is that right?"

BE WHO YOU ARE
YOU MATTER
DON'T LET ANYONE DULL YOUR SPARKLE
CRAYON

Jet nodded, although he wasn't sure whether he would have called what happened in the classroom a misunderstanding. Tim was being generous.

"How about you tell me your version of what happened?"

Jet told Tim what had happened, careful to avoid any mention of Mum or Dad, just saying that he'd been really tired lately, after moving home and school.

"Would you say you're often tired?" Tim asked.

Jet considered. What if this was a trick question? "Only sometimes."

"Would you say that things at home are going okay?" asked Tim.

Jet frowned. "Yes, everything is fine. Why?"

Tim looked at him searchingly.

"Jet, I have a form I'd like you to fill out, if that's okay? It might give us both a better picture of where you're at. It's just a few multiple-choice questions that could help me figure out any ways in which I can support you."

Jet filled out the form. While Tim looked through his answers, Jet gazed out of the window, past the fence and into the park.

There, an old woman threw a ball for her black-and-white border collie. The dog looked young and energetic and kept bounding back to the woman, who seemed to take forever to stoop to retrieve the ball.

"Do you like dogs?"

"Huh?" Jet emerged from his daydream.

"Dogs." Tim pointed through the gap in the posters to the view of the park beyond the schoolyard.

Jet nodded. "I can't have one, though," he blurted. "Mum isn't well enough to look after it at home."

And then there came a horrible squeeze of fear clenching his insides as Jet realised what he had just said.

Chapter 5

Bandit

When the bell rang, Jet was reluctant to return home. Feeling heavy with the knowledge that he might have betrayed Mum by letting it slip that she was sick, he dawdled in the park behind the school.

The old lady had returned. This time, she sat on a bench while the border collie raced about in giddy circles.

When the dog saw Jet approach, it bounded over and leapt up with both paws, knocking Jet straight back onto the grass and licking his face with gusto.

Immediately, the lady was up off the bench. "Bandit! Off him. Get off!"

Jet lay under the crazy dog, laughing at the tickle of its tongue, as the lady helplessly yanked at the dog's collar. "I am so sorry, young man. Bandit's still only a pup in his head."

A small knot of people, including a woman pushing a pram, had now stopped to check that Jet was all right.

Jet should have been embarrassed, but instead he burst into laughter. How long had it been since he had last done that? Truly laughed. How long since he'd felt even a moment of not worrying, just a sense of being happy to be lying flat on his back with a waggy out-of-control dog?

"It's okay – really," said Jet, smiling.

"No, he's very naughty," the woman insisted.

Jet caught the fond look in her eyes and knew that there was not going to be a "consequence" for Bandit.

"The problem is," she continued, "that we inherited him from our daughter when she got a job overseas. He's been very spoiled, and neither I nor my husband is quite strong enough to manage him." She shook her head. "My husband is not well, and although Bandit is so naughty, he just loves the dog to bits."

Jet nodded. He understood all of it, including the sadness in her expression when she spoke about her husband not being well. Jet would love a dog like Bandit – any dog – to bits, too.

The lady straightened and flashed Jet a bright smile. "I'm Eileen," she said. "And this young scamp here is …"

"... Bandit," Jet answered, as the collie dived in once more to lick the entire length of Jet's face.

Jet reluctantly clambered out from beneath Bandit and said goodbye. Mum would be wondering where he was.

When he opened the door and no one was home, Jet felt the familiar squeeze of fear, as if burning ice was running through his gut. He told himself that Mum must be at the hospital. But what if this was the time when she didn't come back?

Then Jet spotted a note on the table, telling him she'd be back late, that he was to go to bed at a decent hour, and there was some money for him to get pizza delivered.

Jet checked his phone. There were two missed voice messages from Dad. He deleted them without listening.

Jet played games on his phone until nearly midnight before he heard the taxi pull up outside. He rushed to help Mum inside. Exhausted, she leant half on Jet, half on her walking stick.

She pretended to be cross. "I thought I'd written that you were to go to bed!"

But he knew she was relieved and grateful for his help. Not as relieved as he was, though, to see her back home again.

Chapter 6

Dogs Are the Best

"Jet, catch it!"

Jet pretended not to hear the sighs of exasperation as he missed the ball and it went flying over the boundary line.

He couldn't understand why some of the kids were still trying. Surely, he'd made it clear that he wasn't interested in making friends.

Who knew if he was even going to be at this school for long, anyway? If something happened to Mum, then where was he going to end up? He couldn't live with Aunty Lisa – she already had too much going on. As for Dad, he hardly imagined Dad would want Jet to come along and ruin his perfect life with Tamara and the baby.

Through the fence, Jet could see Eileen and Bandit. Without thinking, he walked off the pitch. He crossed the field and called to Bandit through the fence.

"Jet!" Ms Pinta called. "Jet, come back!"

Bandit bounded over, enthusiastically swiped licks at Jet, then raced back towards the park.

By the time Ms Pinta arrived, flushed with anger and shaking her head, Jet knew he was in trouble. It was off to the counsellor again …

This time, Tim didn't ask him about home. Instead, he asked Jet about dogs.

"What do you like about them?"

"They're fun," Jet said. "They just love you no matter what. I don't know, I just feel better with dogs."

Tim nodded. "Jet, all these feelings you've been having – the sick feeling in your gut, not being able to concentrate, not wanting to be with other kids, all the worry you're feeling – that's called anxiety." He paused and then added, "And I'm guessing, with what's going on for your mum, you've got some good reasons to be feeling anxious."

"Who said something?" Jet demanded.

Tim's tone was gentle. "You did."

Jet fought back the tears burning behind his eyes. "I don't want to talk about it."

"And you don't have to – that's your right," Tim agreed. "Only, sometimes talking about it with someone else, someone like me, can help."

"How would it help?"

"Well, to start with, it might make you feel less alone."

But you couldn't trust people, Jet knew that. Look how Dad had left when Mum was sick. Look how people, including Mum, pretended she was going to get better, when they didn't really know.

"You know what would make me feel less alone?" Jet asked.

Tim leant forward, eager to hear the answer.

"A dog. Dogs are the best."

Tim nodded. "Maybe you're right. But in the meantime, instead of a dog in my office, you've got me. Woof!"

It was so ridiculous that, despite himself, Jet smiled.

"You can't bottle it up forever, Jet. I think it's time you shared just a little bit of what's making you so unhappy."

Chapter 7

A Surprise

Mum moved her legs off the couch so that she and Jet could share some Indian takeaway.

"I'm sorry I'm not up for cooking," she said. "Do you remember how I used to be obsessed with making everything from scratch?"

Jet nodded as he crunched a poppadom, although truthfully, he couldn't remember eating a home-cooked meal in months. He noticed that Mum ate like a bird, forking up a few grains of rice and a quarter of a mouthful of butter chicken.

"I had a call from the school today," she said.

Jet froze. It was one thing for him to be in trouble at school, but another thing for the school to be bothering Mum about it. The last thing he wanted was her worrying about him.

Mum continued, "From a man named Tim. He sounded very nice."

Jet felt a surge of anger. Tim had told him that he was only required to say something to someone else if he thought Jet was at serious risk of harm.

Otherwise, Tim had promised that what they discussed would not leave his office.

"What did he say?" Jet asked cautiously.

Mum looked at him searchingly. The tired love in her eyes was almost painful. "He's concerned about the pressure on you, starting a new school. He suggested that he'd like you to be part of a program the school is bringing in. He's asked for my permission for you to be one of the first students to test it out."

"What kind of program?"

Jet was astonished to see a sudden light twinkling in Mum's eyes. "Oh, I don't think I should say anything at this point. It's a surprise."

The following day at school, Jet was staring into space, halfway through learning about how the Egyptian pyramids were built, when a student came to the door with a note.

"Jet, you need to go to the office," Ms Pinta instructed.

Had something happened to Mum? Jet's heart pounded. His mouth went dry and there was a familiar burning in his gut. "Do I need to take my things?" he asked.

"No, just leave them here," the teacher said.

Some of the burning subsided. If he was coming back to class, then it meant Mum must be okay.

Tim greeted him at the office. "Just the person I wanted to see. You and I are the welcoming committee."

"Welcoming committee? Who for?"

"Good question," Tim said. "Or, maybe you should be asking *what* for?"

The glass door slid open and a woman came in, preceded by a golden retriever. The dog wore a bright orange dog jacket and wagged its tail as if going to school was the most exciting thing that had ever happened to it.

"Hi, Tim ... and you must be Jet," the woman said, beaming. "I'm Heidi, but more importantly, this is Honey. Honey, say hi to Jet."

Honey lifted a fluffy paw to shake and gazed at Jet with shining brown eyes.

It was instant love.

"Jet, do you know what an emotional support dog is?" asked Heidi.

Jet frowned. "Like a guide dog?"

Heidi smiled. "Close, but those are assistance dogs for people with visual impairments, autism or mobility issues. They get a lot more training, and they're legally allowed in all public places. Emotional support dogs are mostly for helping people to feel calmer, especially when they're feeling anxious or worried."

“What’s this got to do with me?” Jet asked.

“You mentioned that a dog would make you feel better,” Tim said simply. “And to tell the truth, I’ve been itching to get a dog into the school from the moment I heard about emotional support dogs.”

“So, she’s mine?” Jet asked wonderingly.

Tim and Heidi exchanged glances.

“Every day while you’re at school, she will be supporting you,” Heidi said. “I’m going to teach you more about her and hang around with you, to begin with. At the end of each day, she will come home with me, where I promise you that she gets to sleep on the softest bed surrounded by a ridiculous number of toys, and eats only the finest steak,” Heidi added with a smile.

Chapter 8

Honey

Honey was allowed to sit right next to Jet. She had her own special spot beside his desk.

Whenever Jet began to stare out the window or fidget with his pencils, Honey would put her paw on his leg, or gently rest her face against him and nudge him with her cold nose. It was as if she knew when the anxiety was too much and Jet went, as Tim had put it, "offline".

Jet found it soothing to run his fingers through her silky fur. When he started to worry about Mum, Honey seemed to know and leant softly against him.

During recess and lunch, it didn't feel fair to Honey to just sit in the library. Instead, Jet took her outside, and before long other kids were begging him to join their games.

Watching Honey race about for a ball, wagging her tail so hard she almost spun in circles, Jet felt something he hadn't felt in a long while. So long, he hardly recognised what it was. Happiness. Pure, simple happiness.

Because Honey was in the playground, Ms Ravel gave a big speech to the whole school about cleaning up rubbish and making sure that there was never anything lying around that would be bad for Honey if she ate it.

It was a wrench saying goodbye to Honey at the end of each day. Jet always walked Honey to the school gates when Heidi arrived to pick her up. But it meant he couldn't wait to get to school the next day to see her again.

Jet started drawing again. He created cartoon pictures of Honey chasing a football, or Honey reading in a row of kids, wearing a pair of glasses, or Honey sitting on a bench at lunch-time with a sandwich in her paw. When the other kids saw his drawings, they all wanted him to do one of them with Honey, so Jet started to draw portraits.

Jet now realised that for the whole time he'd sat in class, refusing to make friends, he had privately been taking notice of his classmates – what they liked or what made them distinctive. He drew a picture of Oliver and Honey flying paper planes. He did one of Lili and Honey painting – Honey with a paintbrush in her snout. Oliver and Lili were both pleased with the pictures, and later they asked Jet if he'd like to go skateboarding with them after school.

Without noticing it, Jet found that he was making friends. And the more he made friends, the less he minded how, when another student got upset, the teacher asked them to go and sit on the beanbag and read out loud to Honey. It didn't matter what the story was, Honey seemed happy, and eventually so was the kid who'd been sent to read to her in the first place.

Honey always returned straight after to her place beside Jet. She was completely clear that he was her best friend, and she was his. Yet, Jet realised that he was proud of Honey for being able to help other people, too.

Chapter 9

Birthday Cake

"I've been wondering what you'd like to do for your birthday," Mum said.

Jet blinked. He had barely thought about his birthday.

"Would you like to have a party?"

Jet looked around the small house. There would be no room. And he still wasn't comfortable with friends coming back here and seeing how Mum was.

He felt a clutch of fear – was she saying this because she secretly thought it might be the last birthday she would get to attend?

"Maybe I could invite a couple of my friends to the skatepark?" Jet suggested.

Mum nodded, bright-eyed despite her drawn face. "We'll have a cake," she said. "And it won't be from a bakery. I'm going to make it myself."

Jet had to admit that his birthday was actually okay. Dad had phoned that morning with the baby screaming in the background, and he had promised to put money for a new bike into Jet's account. He must have been feeling guilty, because it was a lot more than Jet could have dreamed of.

The skatepark was bathed in sunshine, and Mum and Aunty Lisa had set up a magnificent-looking cake on a picnic rug in the dappled shade beneath a tree.

Jet was doing tricks with Oliver and Lili in the skate bowl when Heidi turned up with Honey. Unleashed, Honey bounded towards Jet with undisguised joy.

Honey then watched from the side of the skate bowl until it was time for cake when, in her excitement, she skidded across the blanket and promptly planted a paw into the cake.

There were gasps as the cake partly toppled, until, at Honey's crestfallen expression, Jet dissolved into laughter.

Jet crammed a slice of cake into his mouth before going back to join Oliver and Lili on the ramp.

As he walked, he gazed around at all the people (and the dog) he loved best.

Of all the things that Honey did and was, for all her loving, waggy ways, something she did so well was to enjoy every moment. And that, Jet thought, was something that right now – even if just for today – he was going to let himself do, too.